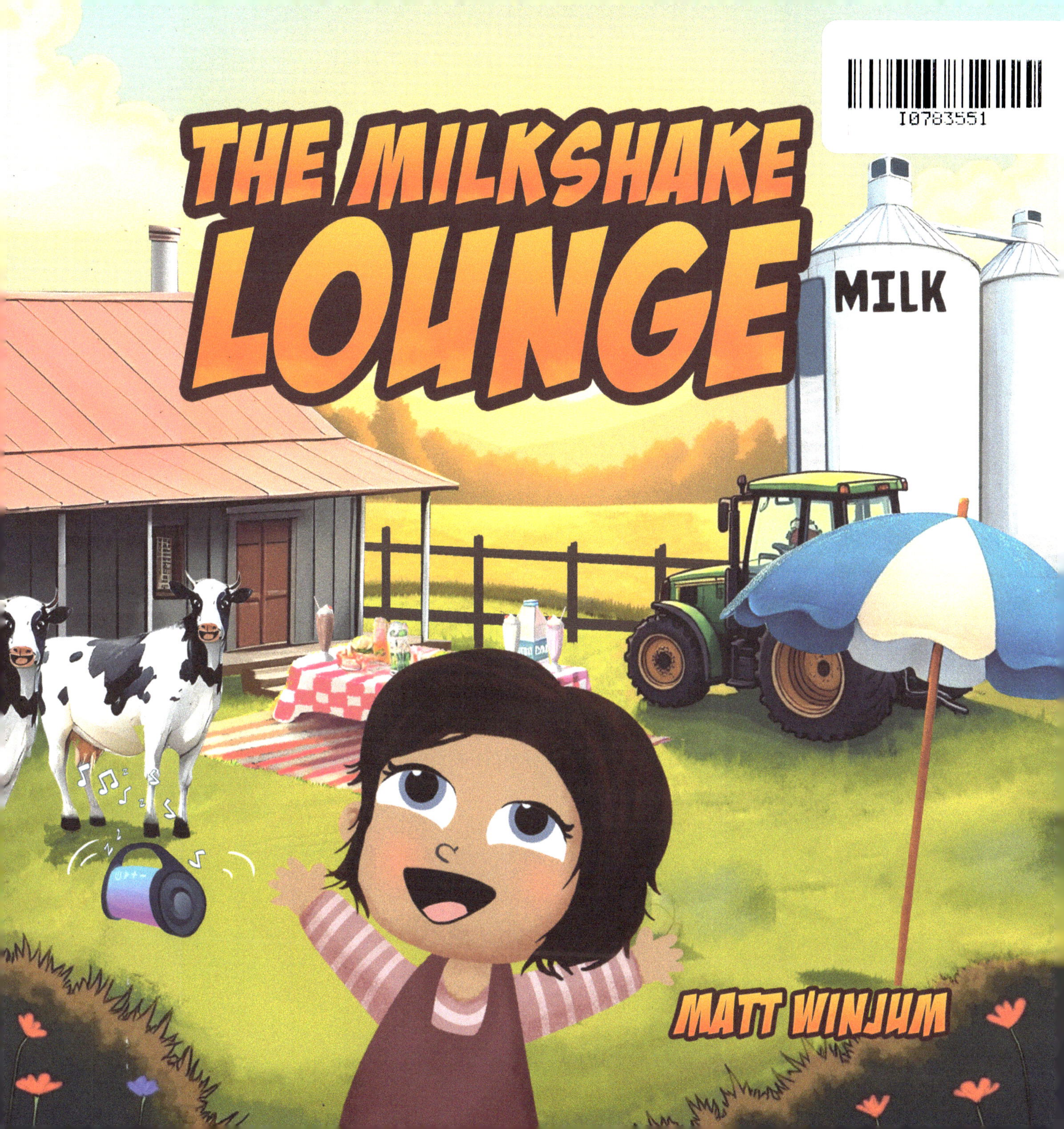
I0783551
THE MILKSHAKE LOUNGE
MILK
MATT WINJUM

"CREATED WITH LOVE FOR MY GENEVIEVE, THEODORE AND KATE. GO TEAM WIN!!"

Mom pleads, "Guys, we gotta go! Our flight to New Zealand leaves soon. Genevieve, eat your food. Don't be rude."

Grandma and Grandpa (papa) are living in New Zealand for six months as papa works as a traveling doctor.
Mom sings, "The bags are all packed, we're ready to go."
Dad joins, "Because we're leaving on a jet plane."
Mom continues, "And this flight is going to be insane."

It takes 17 hours to fly across the world from the USA to New Zealand.

The flight attendant asks, "Can I get you anything, ma'am?"

Mom desperately replies, "Some sleep, please."

Another flight attendant comes and asks, "Can I get you anything, Sir?"

Dad says, smiling, "I'll have another pillow, please. I can't believe this flight is such a breeze."

Papa greeted, "Welcome to New Zealand! How was your flight?"
Dad grinned, "It was a delight!"
Papa asks, "Where are Kate's bags?"
Dad shrugged, "Lost in translation."

The cramped car crunches up the dusty, dirty path. It slowly stops in front of the cute cottage.

Tuakau, New Zealand.

Papa proudly says, "Welcome to Cow Camp! Look, here comes Farmer Francis."

Farmer Francis waves, "Howdy, folks!"

Dad asks, "Is this heaven?" He smiles while admiring the view.

Farmer Francis replies with a laugh, "No, this is Tuakau, New Zealand!"

Farmer Francis leans against the fence, looking at the cows, "We have a lot of friendly faces round here, but someone has been bothering the bovine."

Grandpa asks, "What happens if the cows don't calm down?"

Farmer Francis replies with a frown, "Cranky cows don't make much milk. And no milk means we're in trouble."

MILK

Kooky Kiwi

Funny Pheasant

Pesky Possum

Mom asks Genevieve, "Can you say cow?"
Genevieve tries, "C O O..."
Mom slowly says, "C O W."
Genevieve says, "C O W W."
Farmer Francis chuckled, "Yeah, these are dairy cows. They make milk. But lately, they haven't been making much milk. I think we have a pest problem."

The sun shined brightly as the family gathered on the patio. Milkshakes were on the table, and music played softly from a Bluetooth speaker.

Dad sings, "Sippin on milk shakes, watching the sun bake, all us tourists from the U.S."

Genevieve is loving the trip and learning new words with each tasty sip.

Mom slowly says, "Cows make milkshakes; cows make milkshakes."

Genevieve repeats, "Cows make milkshakes."

Papa says, "I think we will show you Karioitahi this weekend, the black beach."

Papa says, looking at Genevieve, "Genevieve is loving wading in the waves."

Genevieve shouts, "Pwayne, Pwayne. Bwack Beach."

Grandma smiles, "Genevieve sure is learning lots of words."

Mom adds, "Living her best life!"

Genevieve says, "Seashells, Sand, Salt, Surfers."

Genevieve returned from the black beach with lots of seashells from the seashore. The cow's conundrum with making milk has gotten worse.

Farmer Francis asks, "How was the beach?"

Genevieve replies, "Yay! Great!"

MILK

Papa asks, "How are the cows?"

Farmer Francis frowns, "Not making much milk. I don't know what or who is making cranky cows

Mom says, "Wow, the sun is sizzling."

Dad replies, "I'll set up the sun shade". If we had a pool, we'd be made in the shade."

Grandma says, "I'll make milkshakes."

Genevieve claps her hands, "Cows mooooving!"

Papa chuckles, "Ha! Yeah, it looks like they like the music. Let's go to the South Island this weekend."

New Zealand is made up of two islands, the North Island and the South Island. Each island is filled with amazing places to explore.

Grandma asks, "Are you having fun, Genevieve?"
Genevieve shouts, "Yay! Fun!"
Mom adds, "Can you say B O A T?"
Genevieve repeats, "B O A T!"
Papa joins in, "Can you say float?"

Genevieve laughs, "Fwoat!"
Dad playfully asks, "Can you say Goat?"
Genevieve proudly says, "Goat!"

Mom, "Wow! What a wonderful weekend."
Papa, "I wonder how the cows are doing?"

Farmer Francis asks, "Did you have fun in the fjord?"

Genevieve smiles, "Yay! Fun!"

Papa asks, "How are the cows doing?"

Farmer Francis shakes his head, "Not making much milk. We definitely have a pesky problem and cranky cows."

MILK

The night stars in New Zealand are different from those in the United States. The most famous constellation is the Southern Cross.

Mom points to the sky, "Look at the Southern Cross. Isn't it beautiful?"

Grandma agrees, "The stars are stunning."

Farmer Francis adds, "The kiwis and possums really come out at night. They are nocturnal. Possums have been labeled a pest in New Zealand."

Genevieve whispers, "Uh-oh. Pesty problem."

Possums were introduced to New Zealand in 1837 and were officially labeled a pest in 1946. Milk is New Zealand's biggest primary industry export earner.

Farmer Francis, "For as small as New Zealand is, it is a massive milk maker."

Mom says, "Cows make milk."

Genevieve echoes, "Cows make milk. Music make milk."

Grandma says, "Genevieve, your trip is already coming to an end."
Mom asks, "Tell us what you have learned."
Genevieve proudly replies, "Pesky possums, cranky cows, music makes milkshakes."
Papa laughs, "Hahaha! That's it, Genevieve!"

Farmer Francis exclaims, "That's it, Genevieve! You've solved it! The music keeps the cows happy, helps them make more milk, and the pesky possums stay away."

Dad starts singing, "The cows are always moooooooovin to the music at The Milkshake Lounge!"

Genevieve saved the day,
And learned a lot of words to say.
YAY

Enjoying adventures along the way,
This trip really was grade A!
Genevieve exclaims, "Yay!"

The sun is always shining,
The birds are always singing,
The kids are always dancing at
The Milkshake Lounge.
The farmer's always talking,
The tractor's always humming,
The music's always playing at
The Milkshake Lounge.

The Kiwi's always cooing,
The Pheasant's always strutting,
And the cows are always moooooovin to the music at The Milkshake Lounge,
Yeeaaaaahhhh!

Scan the QR code to listen to recordings of The Milkshake Lounge song!
Sang and performed by Joe Eddie